Jasmine CAN

Creating Self-Confidence

Written by Bena Hartman • Illustrated by Mary Gregg Byrne

Ferne Press

Jasmine Can: Creating Self-Confidence
Copyright © 2011 by Bena Hartman
Illustrated by Mary Gregg Byrne
Layout and cover design by Kimberly Franzen and Raphael Giuffrida
Illustrations created with watercolors
Printed in the United States of America

Summary: When a second grader takes a chance in class, her confidence level soars.

Library of Congress Cataloging-in-Publication Data
Hartman, Bena
Jasmine Can: Creating Self-Confidence/Bena Hartman–First Edition
ISBN-13: 978-1-933916-87-3
1. Juvenile fiction. 2. Elementary school. 3. Reading. 4. Self-confidence.
I. Hartman, Bena II. Jasmine Can: Creating Self-Confidence
Library of Congress Control Number: 2011930776

FERNE PRESS

Ferne Press is an imprint of Nelson Publishing & Marketing
366 Welch Road, Northville, MI 48167
www.nelsonpublishingandmarketing.com
(248) 735-0418

To my husband, Doug, who I continually learn from every day.

To my children, Vail, Laya, and Bethany, our independent readers, writers, and thinkers.

To extraordinary teachers everywhere from our past, present, and future.

And of course to my parents, Dr. Charles and Ruth Hefflin, my first teachers.

Thank you to my editors, Kris Yankee and David Nelson; our sessions were a blast.

Special thanks to Jennifer Eddy and her 2009–2010 third-grade classroom. Thanks for inviting me into your class and listening to my stories. You were an amazing audience.

—B. H.

Photo by Amy Phillips

"The best thing about second grade is becoming a better reader," Mom told me.

I think it's the hardest thing about second grade. I mean, why does the letter C have so many sounds? Why is learning to read *so* hard? Does anyone out there know?

No one has to tell Chloe Brown the words when she reads out loud. She knows them all—even the big ones. Why doesn't she make mistakes?

Back in first grade, Mrs. Brennan worked with me every day at the reading table. She held up letters of the alphabet and said, "Jasmine, say the sound."

"Easy peasy," I told her. But it really wasn't easy. I got most of them wrong.

Mrs. Brennan also asked me to read words on cards.
"Easy peasy," I said.
I stared at each word and tried to say the sounds
I heard in my head.

When I thought I could hear all of them together, I'd shout them out. But most of the time I said the wrong word. I always mixed up words like *were* and *where*. And when two vowels went for a walk, I thought they both should talk.

were where

Some days we just read books with a little bit of words on the page. I was embarrassed reading out loud because I read too slowly.

I didn't feel like I was a "real reader."
"A first-grade loser," I'd say to myself. Reading just didn't make sense. I wonder if Chloe ever felt that way.

Mr. Benson is my second grade teacher this year. I still practice reading words every day.

I also read books with a few words on the page with him, too. But we also do different activities.

Like today is fifth-grade buddy day. That's when we read a book with a fifth grader. My buddy's name is Skye.

I love to read with her. She reads smoothly and sounds like a teacher. She even reads chapter books that are over two hundred pages long!

Today I got to choose the book to read with Skye. It was about a baby polar bear.

We looked through the pages, talked about the pictures, and made predictions. Our guesses about the story were pretty close.

In the book, a baby polar bear starts drifting out to sea on a piece of ice. To save himself, he closes his eyes and reaches for his mother, who grabs him safely in her arms.

"You're braver than you think," said Mama.

When we finished the story, we wrote a sentence about something we learned. I wrote, *Sometimes you have to take a chance.*

Before we go home, Mr. Benson usually reads a story to us. But today he asked the class if anyone wanted to read.

Guess who raised her hand first? Chloe Brown. She probably was thinking Mr. Benson would call on her. When I saw her hand, I remembered the little polar bear. *He took a chance.*

For the first time ever, I decided to raise my hand to read in front of my class. My heart skipped a beat, and my throat was dry.

Everyone turned toward me with their mouths wide open.
Mr. Benson said, "Jasmine, come up front to the author's chair."

I stood and carefully made my way to the front of the class and sat down. I had never seen the room from this seat before.

My classmates
sat criss-crossed
applesauce
on the floor
in front of me
while I read
the story about
the baby polar
bear. I read as
smoothly as I
could. If I wasn't
sure of a word,
I looked at the
picture to give
me a clue.

Everyone sat still and listened. I could tell they were just as excited as I was when the baby bear was rescued. When I finished, it was super quiet. Then everyone started cheering and clapping...even Chloe Brown.

When I got home, I shouted, "Mom, I read out loud in front of my whole class!"
She smiled at me and said, "I am so proud of you! And, Mr. Benson is proud of you, too."

I told her it was "easy peasy." Then she gave me the biggest polar bear hug ever.

Now I read every night. I wish
I could say that I'm reading like
Chloe. I know I will someday.

What I can say is that I finally feel like a "real reader!" Reading is beginning to make a lot of sense to me.

My mom is right after all; the best thing about second grade is becoming a better reader. I never knew if the applause that day was for me or the little polar bear.

Oh well, I guess it really doesn't matter…we both had the confidence to say, **"I can!"**

A Note to the Reader

Let's face it: if reading were an easy skill to acquire, there would be no need for this story. The reality is that there are many children just like Jasmine. I wrote this story for two reasons: The first is to give teachers a tool to use in classrooms to inspire the reader inside each of their children. The second is to encourage children, no matter where they are on the ability spectrum, to "take a chance" on becoming better readers.

"All kids are gifted; some just open their packages earlier than others." ~Michael Carr

—B. H.

ABOUT THE AUTHOR

Bena Hartman was born in Nashville, grew up in Pittsburgh, and lives in Okemos, Michigan. She was an elementary school teacher, and later became a university professor. She now holds the title of at-home mom. She drew upon her teaching experiences and childhood memories to write *Jasmine Can: Creating Self-Confidence*. For more information about Bena, please visit her website, www.benahartmanbooks.com.

Photo by James Jablonski

ABOUT THE ILLUSTRATOR

Mary Gregg Byrne lives in Bellingham, Washington. She reads, writes, and creates art. Mary teaches watercolor classes and illustrates children's books. She watches her garden and the children grow. She walks in the mountains. She cherishes her friends. Mary enjoys the changing light of the seasons and of her life. For more information about Mary and her art, please visit www.marygreggbyrne.com.